Stephanie Blake

NOOO!
Not the dentist!

Translated by Linda Burgess

GECKO PRESS

Simon
was invited to
sleep over at
Ferdinand's
house.
Ferdinand's dad
made them
pancakes.

Simon
bit into
his pancake.

"YIIEE!"
he said.
"My tooth hurts,
it really
really
really
hurts!"

"Simon,
you have
a big hole
in your tooth.
Your mother
will need to
take you
to the dentist,"
said Ferdinand's dad.

"Hi, Eva?
Just letting
you know
that Simon has
a big hole
in his back tooth,
and he says
it's very painful."

"Poor old Simon,"
said Ferdinand.
"The dentist
will tie you
to his chair
and force
your mouth open,
then give you a
really really
really
gigantic
injection."

"No way!
I will
NEVER
go to the dentist,"
said Simon.
"I'm Super Rabbit.
And no one gives
Super Rabbit
injections!"

Next morning,
his mother came
to pick him up.

"Hurry up, Simon!"
she said.
"We have
an appointment
with the dentist."

Simon replied,
"The dentist?
No way!"

But his
mother
made him
get into the car
anyway.

"Hey!
It's Super Rabbit!"
said the dentist.

"Poo bum!"
replied Simon.

"Delighted to
meet you, Poo Bum.
My name's Marie.
Come and lie
on my Superchair
for Super Rabbits."

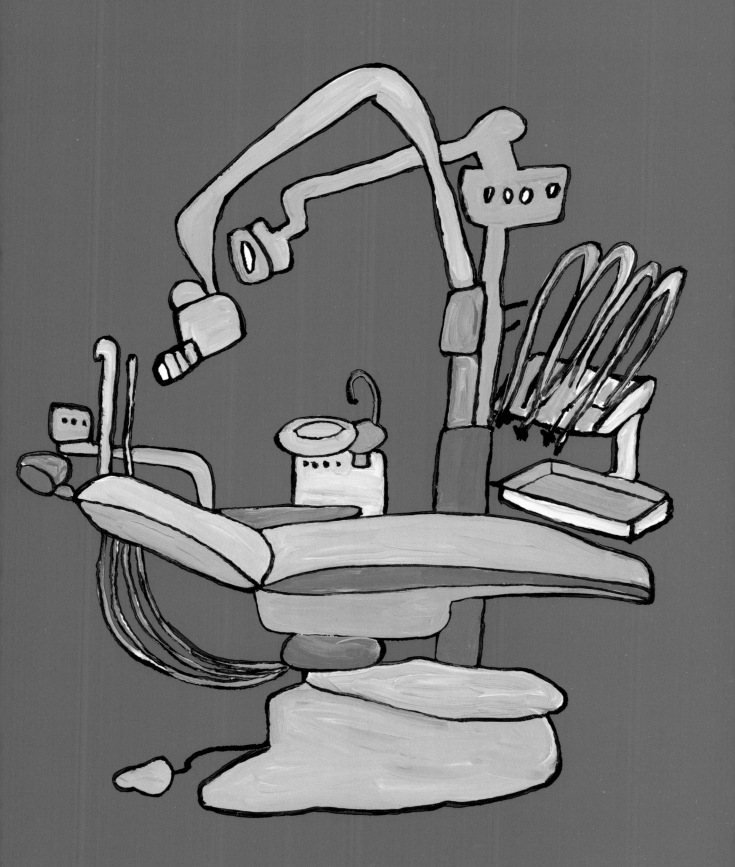

But his
mother
made him
lie on it
anyway.

"Don't worry,"
said Marie.
"This won't hurt."

She put
strawberry paste
in his mouth.
It tasted exquisite.

Simon lay still
and let her
take care
of his tooth.

"There you go,
Poo Bum. All done."

"My name's
Simon," he said.

"Pleased to
meet you,
Simon.
You were very brave."

"Of course,"
said Simon.
"I'm Super Rabbit!"

When Simon
got home,
he called
Ferdinand
to tell him
just one thing:
"It didn't hurt a bit!"

This edition first published in 2023 by Gecko Press
PO Box 9335, Marion Square, Wellington 6141, New Zealand
office@geckopress.com

English-language edition © Gecko Press Ltd 2023
Translation © Linda Burgess 2023
Original title: *Aaaah ! pas le dentiste !*
Text and illustrations by Stephanie Blake © 2010, l'école des loisirs, Paris

Gecko Press is committed to sustainable practice. We publish books to be read over
and over. We use sewn bindings and high-quality production and print all our new books
using vegetable-based inks on FSC-certified paper from sustainably managed forests.

Original language: French
Edited by Penelope Todd
Typesetting by Katrina Duncan
Printed in China by Everbest Printing Co. Ltd, an accredited ISO 14001 & FSC-certified printer

ISBN paperback: 9781776575312

For more curiously good books, visit www.geckopress.com